TANK GIRL

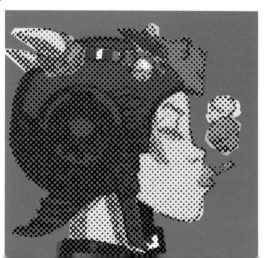

ARTISTS

Jamie Hewlett

Phillip Bond

Glyn Dillon

WRITER

Alan Martin

COLOURISH

Steve Whittaker

DESIGNER

Frank Wynne

FONTOGRAPHER

Rian Huges AT Device

TaNk GIRl III

Jamie Hewlett
& Alan Martin

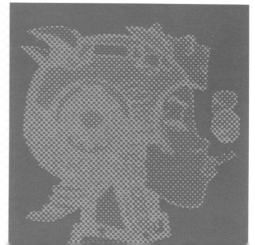

PENGUIN BOOKS

Published by the Penguin Group

Penguin Books Ltd, 27 Wrights Lane, London W8 5TZ, England

Penguin Books USA Inc., 375 Hudson Street, New York, New York 10014, USA

Penguin Books Australia Ltd, Ringwood, Victoria, Australia

Penguin Books Canada Ltd, 10 Alcorn Avenue, Toronto, Ontario, Canada M4V 3B2.

Penguin Books (NZ) Ltd, 182-190 Wairau Road, Auckland 10, New Zealand

Penguin Books Ltd, Registered Offices: Harmondsworth, Middlesex, England

First published in Deadline Magazine from 1992 to 1995

Published in Penguin Books 1996

1 3 5 7 9 10 8 6 4 2

Printed in England by William Clowes Ltd, Beccles, Suffolk NR34 9QE

PENGUIN BOOKS

CONTENTS

BY LATE AFTERNOON WE HAD KILLED EVERYONE EXCEPT JACKIE MARROW. WE CHANGED CLOTHES AND POPPED INTO THE AUTHENTIC NINETEENTH CENTURY COWBOY SALOON WHICH HAD BEEN BUILT SPECIALLY FOR THE CONVENTION SO THAT MACHO DING DONGS COULD STAGE FAKE STUNT SHOOT-OUTS FOR PRE-PUBESCANT BASTARDS. WE SWIGGED RED-EYE, BLUE-EYE AND JAP'S-EYE, SMOKED BIG BROWN CIGARS AND PLANNED OUR FINAL SHOOT-OUT WITH THE MEANEST BOUNTY HUNTER OF THEM ALL...

WHEN WE SMELT HIS APPROACH I MADE LIKE THE INVISIBLE MAN. TANKGIRL STAYED FOR THE TOSSING OF THE GAUNTLET.

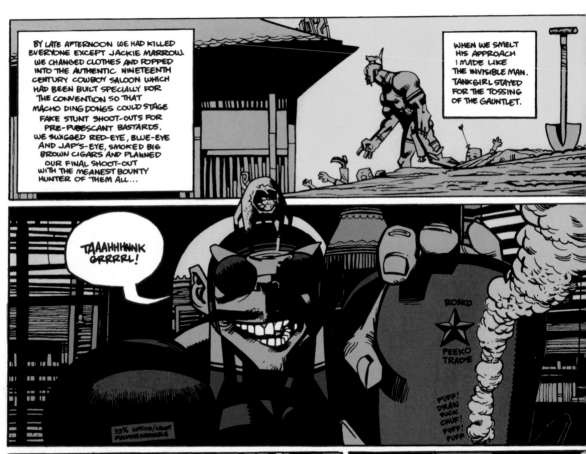

TAAAHHHNNK GRRRRL!

ROSKO
PEEKO TRADE

PUFF!
DRAW
SUCK
CHUF!
PUFF!
PUFF

99% COTTON/GRUMP MACHINE WASHABLE

THAT'S MY NAME ...

DON'T WEAR IT OUT!

MEEET MEEE IN THE STREEET IN ONE MEEENUTE!

HOPE BOOGA'S IN POSITION!

$5

THE END

SPECIAL THANKS TO ROGER MOORE.

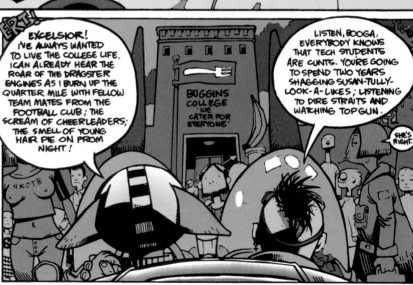

AFTER TWO WEEKS OF TRYING TO TEACH BOOGA TO COOK 'LEAN CUISINE', THE STAFF SEND HIM TO THE WORKSHOP WHERE HE MEETS COLLEGE BAD BOYS PETE DIGGLE AND STEVE SHELLEY. FOR THEIR END OF TERM PROJECT THEY MAKE A PERFECT REPLICA OF A 1963 FENDER TELECASTER.

IT'S FUCKING GREAT, BOOGA, IT'S THE SMOOTHEST GUITAR I'VE EVER SEEN. YOU SHOULD BE PROUD!

CHEERS FELLAS, I COULDN'T HAVE DONE IT WITH-OUT YOUR HELP!

C'MON, LET'S GO TO THE COMMON-ROOM AND WE'LL TEACH YOU TO PLAY 'HARMONY IN MY HEAD!'

A YEAR AND A HALF LATER...

HOW DID IT GO, BOOGA? WHAT DID THEY TEACH YOU?

WELL, I LEARNED HOW TO MAKE A POT NOODLE; I'VE GOT KEN HOLM'S ADDRESS; AND I MADE THIS GUITAR AND MY MATES SHOWED ME HOW TO PLAY 'HARMONY IN MY HEAD'.

MOVE OVER DANDO

I'LL GIVE YOU HARMONY IN YOUR FUCKING HEAD!!

EARTH?

SNATCH!

YOU BURK!

CRUNCH!

OW!

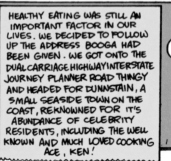

HEALTHY EATING WAS STILL AN IMPORTANT FACTOR IN OUR LIVES. WE DECIDED TO FOLLOW UP THE ADDRESS BOOGA HAD BEEN GIVEN. WE GOT ONTO THE DUAL CARRIAGE HIGHWAY INTERSTATE JOURNEY PLANNER ROAD THINGY AND HEADED FOR DUNNSTAIN, A SMALL SEASIDE TOWN ON THE COAST, REKNOWNED FOR IT'S ABUNDANCE OF CELEBRITY RESIDENTS, INCLUDING THE WELL KNOWN AND MUCH LOVED COOKING ACE, KEN!

GO!

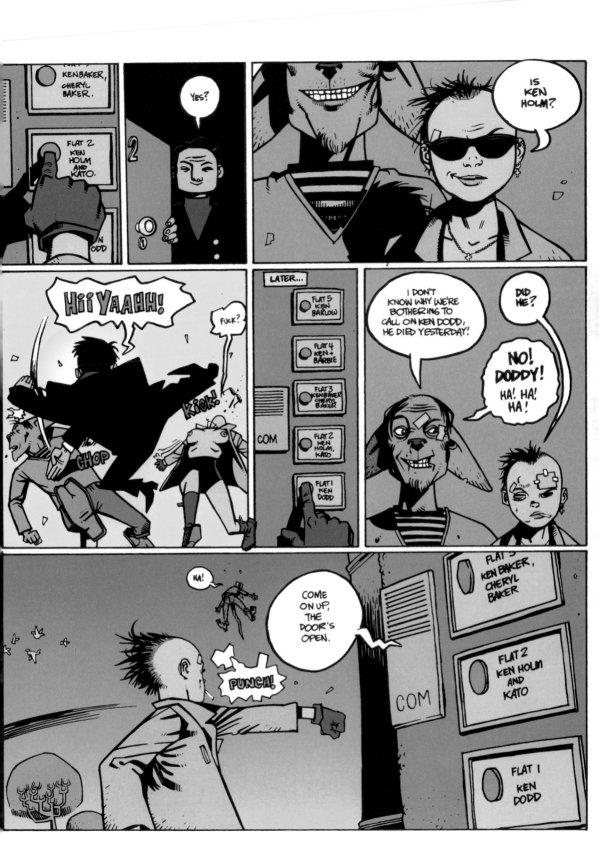

the IMMORTALISTS

ONE SUNNY DAY NEAR THE LOCAL GRAVEYARD....

JUST STOP RIGHT THERE IN YOUR TRACKS TUCKER. DON'T YOU THINK IT'S ABOUT TIME YOU STOPPED PLAYING WITH ALL OF THAT WORLD WAR TWO SHIT?

WHAT DO YOU MEAN, DOYLE?

I'M TALKING ABOUT ALL OF THAT STUFF YOU KEEP IN YOUR GRANDADS GASMASK CASE UNDER YOUR BED.... THE RATION BOOK, THE VICTORIA CROSS, THE BULLETS AND THAT LIVE GRENADE - ALL OF THAT CRAP.

THAT STUFF IS MY FLIPPIN' LIFE BLOOD, YOU NUTTER. I'LL ALWAYS CHERISH IT, MY GRANDAD WAS A HERO.

YOU SHOULDN'T TIE YOURSELF TO ALL OF THAT OLD TAT - NOW THAT WE'VE DONE GRANGE HILL WE'RE FUCKING IMMORTAL. WE'RE FUCKING INDESTRUCTABLE!

YOU'RE RIGHT! I'M TUCKER FUCKING JENKINS! ROLE MODEL TO THE COMPREHENSIVE GENERATION!

I AM KING! I AM GOD!

I AM THE NUTJOB!

FUCKING YES!

GREAT! HERE COME ALAN AND BENNY!

LISTEN LADS, WE'RE ALL GOING TO LIVE FOREVER!

HOLD YOUR HORSES! MR. BAXTER FOUND OUT THAT WE'VE ALL BEEN SMOKING IN THE BOILER ROOM... AND HE'S COMING DOWN THE ROAD, RIGHT NOW!

FLIPPIN'ECK! LEGGIT!

NEXT MONTH : FLIPPIN'ECK BENNY YOU NUTJOB.

A STRING OF HITS ENSUED, INCLUDING THE BLOCKBUSTING 'HEAVEN KNOWS I'M MORRISSEY NOW', THE CONTROVERSIAL 'HANDSOME NEVILLE', THE FOOTSTOMPING 'PICNIC' AND 'GIRLFRIEND IN A COMMERVAN', A SONG INSPIRED BY THE T.V. SHOW 'THE LIVER BIRDS'.

CAKEHOLE, WHY DON'T YOU SHUT YOUR CAKEHOLE HU HU HU HA HA! ♫

INEVITABLY, A STRING OF SELL OUT CONCERTS, OR 'GIGS' AS THE FANS KNEW THEM, TOOK THEIR TOLL ON THE BAND - PARTICULARLY ON MORRISSEY, WHO SUFFERED A DEBILITATING EAR INFECTION AGGRAVATED BY THE VOLUME OF JONNY'S AMPLIFIED ELECTRIC GUITAR.

DURING MORRISSEY'S SOJOURN, SIXTIES CHANTEUSE AND LONG-TIME HEROINE OF THE BAND'S, ANITA HARRIS TOOK OVER ON VOCALS...

AND A HIT T.V. SERIES ENDEARED THE SMITHS TO A NEW GENERATION OF FANS.

IT WAS TWO YEARS BEFORE MORRISSEY RETURNED TO THE STAGE, BUT IN WHAT STYLE! THE NEW ALBUM 'THE QUEEN IS DEAF' WAS A WORLDWIDE SUCCESS. THE SMITHS WERE FINALLY BIGGER THAN GOD; MORRISSEY WAS THE MOST RESPECTED AND WELL PAID POP STAR IN HISTORY.

Uh... Pardon?

SONGS LIKE 'SHOPFITTERS OF THE WORLD', 'ASK ASPEL', 'THE BOY WITH THE SIZEABLE THORN' AND 'I STARTED SINGING AND COULDN'T FINISH' WERE STUDIED IN UNIVERSITIES AND BECAME ANTHEMS FOR A GENERATION.

YET, DESPITE HIS FABULOUS RICHES, MORRISSEY REFUSED TO BECOME DETACHED FROM THE WORLD'S TROUBLES. THE BESPECTACLED SINGER WOULD NOT REST UNTIL HE'D ORGANISED AND HEADLINED A MASSIVE BENEFIT CONCERT FEATURING THE WHO, QUEEN, THE BEATLES AND STATUS QUO.

THE SMITHS SAVED THE WORLD.

A VICAR WITH A YOYO, O-HO. ALL A BIT STRANGE...

BUT ALL WAS NOT QUIET IN THE SMITHS CAMP. JONNY FELT RESTRAINED AND RESTLESS. HE WANTED TO EXPERIMENT IN THE NEW AVANT GARDE ACID TECHNO MOVEMENT. MORRISSEY, MEANWHILE, WAS DRAWN TO THE ROCKABILLY SOUND OF THE FIFTIES.

INEVITABLY, THE SMITHS SPLIT...

AS JONNY FOUND SUCCESS AS KEYBOARDS-WIZARD IN ELECTRO-FUNK COMBO NEW ORDER, MORRISSEY, REJECTED AND ON THE REBOUND, SIGNED A LUCRATIVE FIFTY YEAR CONTRACT AT CAESAR'S PALACE, LAS VEGAS.

HANG ON, PRECOCIOUS - DIDN'T ONE OF THEM DIE OF A HEART ATTACK IN A CAR CRASH BEFORE THEY HIT VEGAS?

NO NO, MY DEAR- YOU'RE THINKING OF THAT BLOKE FROM HUE AND CRY.

...AND THAT'S ANOTHER STORY!

THE END

JAMIE ALAN AND MARTIN HEWLETT's TANKGIRL

BALL HANGER

TANK GIRL

AND THERE IT WAS. THE LAST STONE. EVERYTHING WAS READY.

RIGHT, IF LITTLE DAVID WOULD LIKE TO SIT NEXT TO SUZIE, AND ROWAN CAN GO BETWEEN STUART AND PETER.

HAS EVERYBODY GOT JELLY? CHOW DOWN, KIDS, MUSICAL FISH AFTER THIS.

MAUREEN, I THINK DUNCAN'S PISSED HIMSELF, BUT I CAN'T CATCH HIM. HE KEEPS DIVING BEHIND THE SOFA.

YES, SALLY. THAT'S A LOVELY WOODLOUSE.

IS THAT YOURS? ARE YOU SURE? WELL IT'S NOT MINE. I WOULDN'T BE SEEN DEAD IN THAT.

IT'S FUCKING HORRIBLE. ALL THOSE SHAGGY BITS HANGING OFF THE BOTTOM, AND THE PUFFY SHOULDERS. IT'S GROSS.

IT MUST BE YOURS, YOU SAD OLD FUCK.

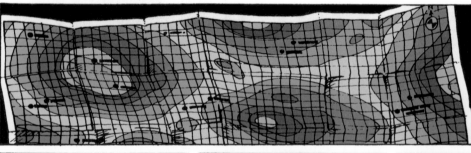

ONE ROCK FROM EACH SECTION ON THE MAP, FORMING A TOWER IN THE CENTER OF THE AREA. THIS WAS HER MISSION OR WAS IT TESTING FOR RADIOACTIVITY? WHO KNOWS ANYMORE. IT WAS SUCH A LONG TIME AGO. THE BOOZE, DRUGS AND INTENSE HEAT HAD ALL TAKEN THEIR TOLL. NO ONE TO TALK TO BUT HER-SELF, THINGS WERE COMING TO A HEAD.

LATER, IN THE JET, THINGS HAD COME TO A HEAD.

FUCK.

YOU'RE FRIENDS WITH ROD STEWART AREN'T YOU? THAT MUST BE REALLY FUCKING COOL.

I'D LOVE TO MEET HIM. I'VE HEARD ALL OF HIS RECORDS. HE'S REALLY FUCKING COOL.

I LOVE ALL OF THAT OLD SHIT HE SINGS ABOUT.

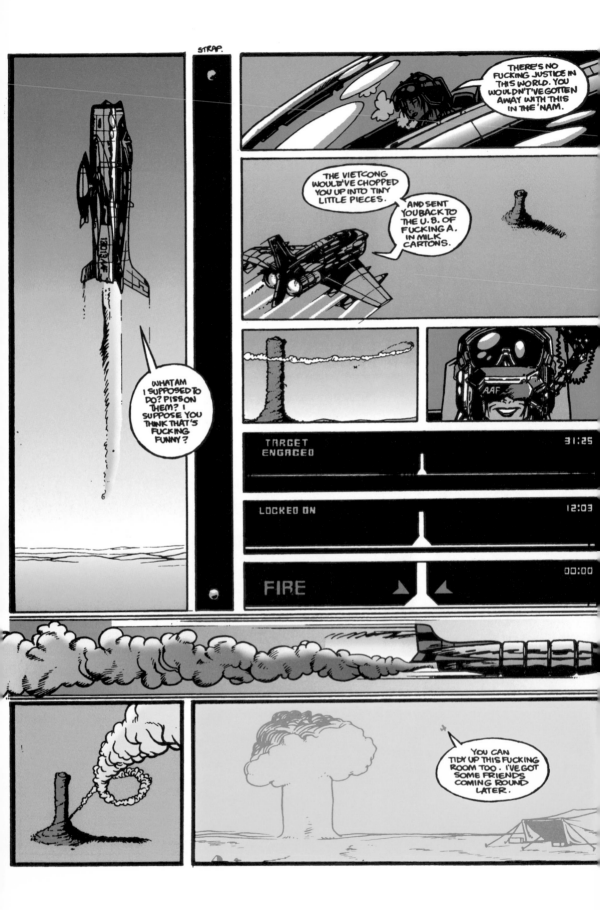

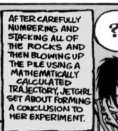

PAGE 23
GLAMOUR BOYS!

JAMIE HEWLETT AND ALAN
"MAJOR LEAGUE" MARTIN
CREATORS OF TANK GIRL
AND MANY OTHER GOOFY
COMIC STRIPS ARE THIS
MONTHS PIN-UP GEEZERS.
JAMIE, AGE 24 LIKES
LYING DOWN, JUMPING,
PORK PIES, BIG BIRD
FROM SESAME STREET
AND GREEN COTTON
UNDERPANTS. HIS FAVE
FOOD GRUB STUFF IS
CHEESE HIS FAVE
COLOUR IS CHEESE
AND HIS BEST POP BAND
IS MIKE AND THE MECHANICS.
ALAN, AGE 36, LIKES
SALVADOR DALI, BRYAN
ADAMS AND GIRLS WITH
BIG TITS. HIS FAVE FOOD
IS CHEESE AND HIS BEST
POP BAND ARE GUNS AND
ROSES. ALAN SAYS HE
WANTS TO ONE DAY OWN
HIS OWN OWNING SHOP
ON THE KINGS ROAD !!!!
CHEERS LADS !...

WHEAT
CHUDLEYS

CEREAL EATER

JAMIE
(NOT FLAVOUR
OF THE MONTH
HEWLETT
92

STARTSMOKING.

MY FRIEND BARNEY IS A FUCKING HEAD CASE, I MET HER IN A MENTAL HOSPITAL. SHE LIKES TO STEEL CARS AND DRIVES LIKE A FUCKING IDIOT. ONE OF THESE DAYS SHE'LL END UP IN STOKE MANDEVILLE SMOKING CIGAR BUTTS WITH JIMMY SAVILLE. I FEEL CLOSE TO HER, WE'VE HAD SO MANY NEAR DEATH EXPERIENCES TOGETHER, WE'VE BONDED ON A VERY STRANGE LEVEL OF CONSCIOUSNESS. MOST OF THE TIME SHE HANGS OUT WITH ALL OF OUR MATES AND SMOKES POT, BUT SOMETIMES SHE SINGLES ME OUT FOR ONE OF HER TRIPS. I ALWAYS GO. HER FAVE FOOD IS TEA AND HER FAVE FILM STAR IS JAMES DEAN. SHE'S NOT RIGHT IN THE HEAD, THAT'S WHY SHE'S NEVER BEEN FUCKED.

FUCKING MY FRIEND.

I've JUST FUCKED MY FRIEND, OF 8 YEARS.
BEHIND ROBBY WILSON'S OLD RUSTY
BULLDOZER. WE'VE NEVER FUCKED BUT
HAVE ALWAYS LOVED EACH OTHER.
IF BOOGA FOUND OUT, HE'D KILL ME AND
THEN KILL HIMSELF.
HE PLAYS LIKE A KID, I REMIND
MYSELF OF HOW SHE TOUCHED ME. ON
MY TITS AND ON MY FUZZ, IT WILL BE
OUR BEST KEPT SECRET, WE WON'T
TELL ANYONE BUT WE'LL WANT TO
TELL EVERYONE, IT WILL PROBABLY
NEVER HAPPEN EVER AGAIN, BUT
THAT'S OK, BECAUSE IT HAPPENED.

THE
HEWLL
93

GAVIN THE FLEABAG!

I DO SOMETHING SPECIAL ON FRIDAY AFTERNOONS. THE REST OF THE
WEEK I HANG AROUND WITH THE GANG, WE RIDE OUR BIKES ON THE
PAVEMENT, SET LIGHT TO OUR PUBES, STEAL, LIE, BREAK THINGS,
SMOKE FAGS DOWN TO THE BUTT, DRAW NOBS ON MODELS IN SKY
MAGAZINE, PUNCH PEOPLE AND SOMETIMES WE CRUISE INTO THE
McDRIVE-IN OF McDONALDS AND ORDER A McSPUNK SHAKE, THEN
WE CALL THEM McCUNTS AND McPETROL BOMB THE McFUCKING JOINT.
BUT ON FRIDAY AFTERNOON I GO AND PLAY WITH MY FRIEND 'GAVIN THE
FLEABAG'. I NEVER TELL ANYONE WHERE I AM, SOMETIMES I SAY IM GOING
TO SEE MY GYNAECOLOGIST, THEN NO ONE PROBES ME BECAUSE SOMETHING
SMELLS FISHY. MY SPECIAL TIME WITH GAVIN IS SPENT PRESSING
FLOWERS, PRANCING, PLAYING DOCTORS AND NURSES, MENDING THINGS,
LISTENING TO 'THE LAMB LIES DOWN ON BROADWAY' BY GENESIS, CRYING,
PLAYING BLOW FOOTBALL AND SOMETIMES WE GO OUT TO THE BACK GARDEN
WITH NO PANTS ON AND JUMP OVER THE GARDEN SPRINKLER. WHEN
IM WITH MY FRIENDS AND I SEE GAVIN, I BLANK HIM.

GLYN.

THIS IS MY FRIEND GLYN, WE WENT TO SCHOOL TOGETHER, WE LIKED 'THE JAM' AND 'THE WHO' AND WE BOTH HAD SCOOTERS. WE BEAT UP ON SQUARES AND SMOKED VANGUARD CIGARETTES. I HADNT SEEN HIM IN 10 YEARS, BUT I COULD TELL BY HIS TRANSLUCENT COMPLEXION, HIS DARK EYELIDS AND HIS SHIT CLOTHES, THAT WE STILL HAD A LOT IN COMMON. HE LIKES TOM WAITS, AL PACINO AND DRUGS. WE BOTH AGREE THAT 'SUEDE' ARE SHIT AND PORNOGRAPHY IS HOT. ITS BEEN 10 MONTHS SINCE OUR LAST MEETING BUT I KNOW WHEN I SEE HIM NEXT HE'LL KNOW.

PARTNERS.

WHEN I FIRST SAW BOOGA HE TRIED IT ON, SO I SAID,"DON'T YOU COME WALKING OVER TO ME LOOKING LIKE AN UNDERAGE RODDY McDOWE HE HADN'T HAD MUCH EXPIERIENCE WITH GIRLS. I THINK I WAS HIS FIRST GIRLFRIEND AND THAT REALLY FREAKED HIM OUT. I TRIED TO KILL HIM ONCE BUT IT DIDN'T WORK. HE DOESN'T TALK ABOUT THAT MUCH, HE PRETENDS IT'S COOL. SOMETIMES I THINK WE HAVE A TELEPATHIC LINK. HE KNOWS TO DUCK WHEN I THROW A WOBBLER. HE KNOWS HOW TO MAKE MY TEA JUST RIGHT. HE'S GOOD AT SQUAT THRUSTS AND RUNNING. AND HE PLAYS A CUNNING GAME OF OTHELLO.

THE HEWLL

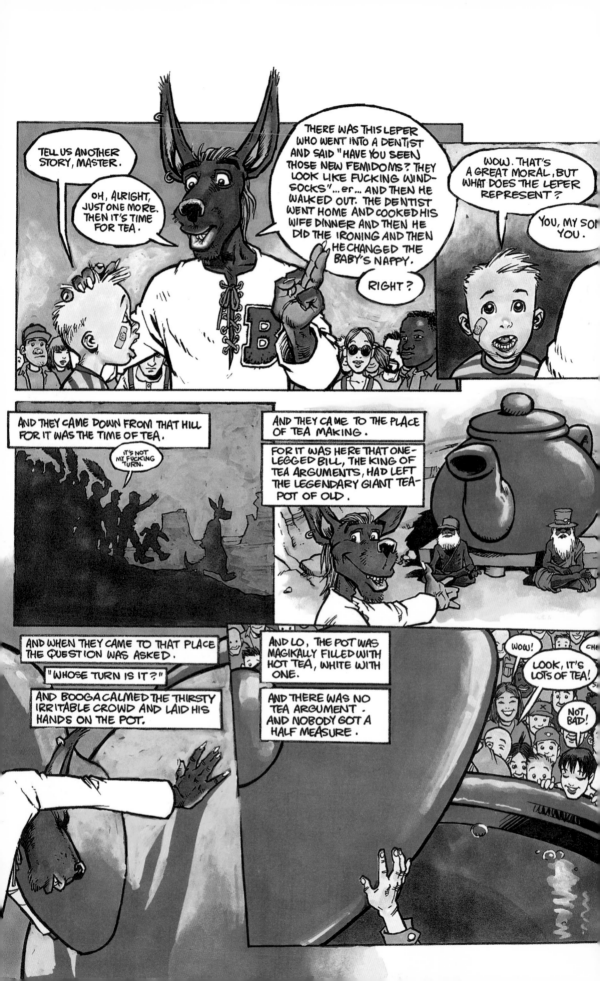

AS THE OTHER REVELLERS FROM THE FEAST RETURNED TO THEIR WIVES, CHILDREN, CHURCHES AND DWELLING PLACES, BOOGA FOUND HIMSELF WANDERING OUT INTO THE WILDERNESS OF THE AUSTRALIAN OUTBACK.

FUCK ME. I FEEL LIKE SHIT.

BEFORE LONG HE WAS TOTALLY LOST. HE DIDN'T KNOW WHICH WAY WAS UP.

I COULD MURDER A COLD BEER.

HE SAT ON THE STONE FOR ELEVEN DAYS AND ELEVEN HOURS.

HIS MIND WAS COMPLETELY CLEAR OF ANY THOUGHT.

AND THEN IT CAME TO HIM. A SONG FROM LONG, LONG AGO. A LYRIC THAT PUT EVERYTHING INTO PERFECT CRYSTAL CLEAR PERSPECTIVE. AND HE HUMMED.

THEY WON'T COME BACK YOU KNOW IT'S ALWAYS THE SAME AND THEY'RE SURE TO FORGET SAYING EVERYONE LIES

SO I'M DOWN TO THIS I'M DOWN TO WALKING ON AIR AND YOU'RE HERE BY MY SIDE WITH ALL YOUR WAVING AND SMILES

PLEASE KEEP THEM AWAY DON'T LET THEM TOUCH ME PLEASE DON'T LET THEM LIE DON'T LET THEM SEE ME ✳

IT IS FINISHED.

eep eep eep!

10:23 AM

AL

OFF   SNOOZE   ALARM   ON   OFF

FROM 'COMPLEX' BY GARY NUMAN ON BEGGARS BANQUET RECORDS

42

43

AT THE BEGINNING OF A NEW YEAR I LIKE TO BUY COPIUS AMOUNTS OF HARD CORE NARCOTICS FROM MY GOOD PAL AND DODGEY DEALER 'EASY ANDY' IN RETURN FOR HIS WARES I DRESS UP AS JACK NICHOLSON AND EAT COLESLAW OFF OF HIS BOLLOCKS WITH A PLASTIC PICNIC FORK.

FEBRUARY 94

M	T	W	T	F	S	S
	1	2	3	4	5 CAR BOOT SALE	6 ROB LOCAL CHEMIST
7 RENT STIMPY 6.25	8	9	10	11	12	13 SYD BARRET BIRTHDAY

GO TO NAVYLINE FOR A TUB OF COLESLAW.

| 14 | 15 | 16 | 17 | 18 | 19 | 20 SIDNEY POITIERS BIRTHDAY |
| 21 | 22 KENNETH WILLIAMS BIRTHDAY | 23 FUCK OFF DAY! | 24 | 25 GEORGE HAMILTON DAY | 26 | 27 |
| 28 |

NOTES: DENTIST FOR INJECTIONS IN MY GUMS! CHEERS!

MARCH 94

M	T	W	T	F	S	S
	1	2 WASH YOUR PRIVATES	3 DR SEUSS DAY	4	5	6 MUMS HOUSE FOR DINNER
7	8	9	10 KILL SOME PEOPLE!	11	12 GET DONE!	13
14 MIKE CAINE DAY	15 GO TO LONDON	16 IN LONDON	17 BACK FROM LONDON	18 BE ILL	19	20
21	22 STEVE DILLONS BIRTHDAY	23	24 STEVE MCQUEENS BIRTHDAY.	25	26	27
28	29	30	31

NOTES: DON'T PAY ANY RENT TO ANYONE, AND SHOOT THE LANDLORD!

APRIL 94

M	T	W	T	F	S	S
SNIFF COKE AND PEPSI				1 BOOGA'S BIRTHDAY CASANOVA BIRTHDAY ALEC GUINNESS	2	3 JAMIE'S B-DAY
4	5	6	7 RABISHANKAR'S BIRTHDAY.	8	9	10
11	12	13	14 JULIE CHRISTIE	15	16 HOFMANN'S BIKE TRIP	17
18	19	20 HITLER HAROLD LLOYD	21 LESLIE PHILLIPS BIRTHDAY	22	23	24
25 AL PACINOS BIRTHDAY	26	27	28 JACK NICHOLSONS BIRTH DAY!	29	30

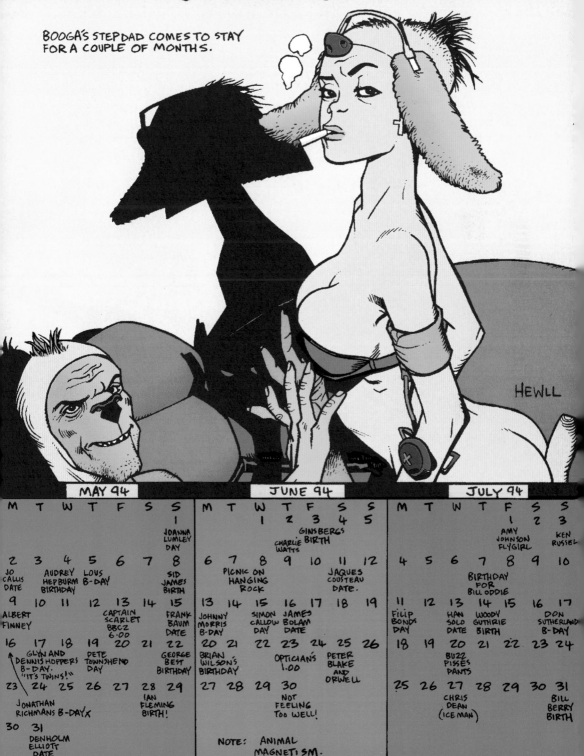

SEX SEASON

BOOGA'S STEPDAD COMES TO STAY FOR A COUPLE OF MONTHS.

HEWLL

MAY 94

M	T	W	T	F	S	S
						1 JOANNA LUMLEY DAY
2 JO CALLIS DATE	3	4 AUDREY HEPBURN BIRTHDAY	5 LOUS B-DAY	6	7	8 SID JAMES BIRTH
9 ALBERT FINNEY	10	11	12	13 CAPTAIN SCARLET BBC2 6.00	14	15 FRANK BAUM DATE
16 GLYN AND DENNIS HOPPERS B-DAY. "IT'S TWINS!"	17	18	19 PETE TOWNSHEND DAY	20	21	22 GEORGE BEST BIRTHDAY
23	24 JONATHAN RICHMANS B-DAY x	25	26	27	28 IAN FLEMING BIRTH!	29
30	31 DENHOLM ELLIOTT DATE					

JUNE 94

M	T	W	T	F	S	S
		1	2	3 GINSBERGS BIRTH	4	5 CHARLIE WATTS
6	7	8 PICNIC ON HANGING ROCK	9	10	11 JAQUES COUSTEAU DATE.	12
13 JOHNNY MORRIS B-DAY	14	15 SIMON CALLOW DAY	16 JAMES BOLAM DATE	17	18	19
20 BRIAN WILSON'S BIRTHDAY	21	22	23 OPTICIANS 1.00	24	25 PETER BLAKE AND ORWELL	26
27	28	29	30 NOT FEELING TOO WELL!			

NOTE: ANIMAL MAGNETISM.

JULY 94

M	T	W	T	F	S	S
				1 AMY JOHNSON FLYGIRL	2	3 KEN RUSSEL
4	5	6	7	8 BIRTHDAY FOR BILL ODDIE	9	10
11 FILIP BONDS DAY	12	13 HAN SOLO DATE	14 WOODY GUTHRIE BIRTH	15	16	17 DON SUTHERLAND B-DAY
18	19	20 BUZZ PISSES PANTS	21	22	23	24
25	26	27 CHRIS DEAN (ICE MAN)	28	29	30	31 BILL BERRY BIRTH

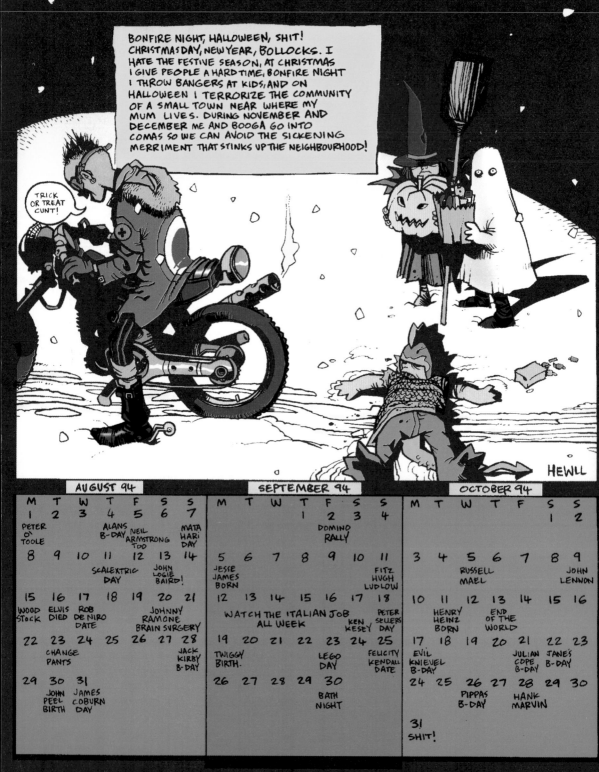

HEWLL

AUGUST 94

M	T	W	T	F	S	S
1	2	3	4	5	6	7
PETER O'TOOLE		ALANS B-DAY	NEIL ARMSTRONG TOO			MATA HARI DAY
8	9	10	11	12	13	14
		SCALEXTRIC DAY			JOHN LOGIE BAIRD!	
15	16	17	18	19	20	21
WOODSTOCK	ELVIS DIED	ROB DE NIRO DATE			JOHNNY RAMONE BRAIN SURGERY	
22	23	24	25	26	27	28
	CHANGE PANTS					JACK KIRBY B-DAY
29	30	31				
JOHN PEEL BIRTH	JAMES COBURN DAY					

SEPTEMBER 94

M	T	W	T	F	S	S
			1	2	3	4
				DOMINO RALLY		
5	6	7	8	9	10	11
JESSE JAMES BORN					FITZ HUGH LUDLOW	
12	13	14	15	16	17	18
WATCH THE ITALIAN JOB ALL WEEK					KEN KESEY	PETER SELLERS DAY
19	20	21	22	23	24	25
TWIGGY BIRTH.				LEGO DAY		FELICITY KENDALL DATE
26	27	28	29	30		
				BATH NIGHT		

OCTOBER 94

M	T	W	T	F	S	S
					1	2
3	4	5	6	7	8	9
		RUSSELL MAEL				JOHN LENNON
10	11	12	13	14	15	16
	HENRY HEINZ BORN		END OF THE WORLD			
17	18	19	20	21	22	23
EVIL KNIEVEL B-DAY				JULIAN COPE B-DAY	JANES B-DAY	
24	25	26	27	28	29	30
		PIPPAS B-DAY		HANK MARVIN		
31						
SHIT!						

The Hewll with son Denholm.

B I O
G R A
P H Y

Alan Martin

Since being thrown off the Tank Woman project for the uncontrolled lack of consideration for others, Alan Martin has worked on a string of World War II movies, notably "G.I. Nose", "Bong over Rubberneck Quarry", and the $80million actioner "Von Ryan's Excuse", as yet unfilmed. Alan's inability as a script writer bodes ill for him in the world outside comics, but his bouncy enthusiasm and undeniable talents in the kitchen make him a literary talent to be reckoned with. The last time I spoke to him was four years ago, outside of a disused jonny factory in Worthing; his parting words wre: "I know this may sound a bit strange, but really we're the same person, y'know?" Yes, Alan, I think I do know.

Hank Chutley, Bovington Tank Museum, Dorset.